Sierra Leone

In

The

Diaspora

A collection of Poems

By

BEE

Aka

Ella Llewelyn Jones

I was also a keen distance runner.

Forward

I'm BOJ a British Sierra Leonean Poet who also writes under the pseudonym, Ella Llewelyn Jones.

I started writing under a pseudonym when I worked as a Special Police Constable in the Metropolitan Police.

My anthology addresses themes such as social injustice, women's rights, black history, and corruption in African politics. This collection isa poignant look at the social and political circumstances of women in Sierra Leone.

I'm an English Language and Literature graduate who later went on to study Criminology and Social Sciences.

I'm a mum to a lovely boy who suffers with Autism.

Contents Page

22. That Black Girl

23. Reflect The Real Me

24. A War Memorial

25. Sierra Leone, A Rough Diamond

26. Christmas Romance

27. Freedom Fled Freetown

28. Sherbro's Shackles

29. Leema Had the Hump

30. Sabanoh's Classic

31. Culture War

32. My Maternal Message

33. They Call Her Madam Cole

34. Misogyny's Rainbow

35. Ode To Leone Stars

36. Freetown Will Be Free

37. Ground nut Seller

38. Polygamy's Enemy

A Hidden Bush

(A poem on Female Genital Mutilation/FGM)

The dark silhouettes in the bush

Hold a secret

Of a practice indiscreet

Innocent girls file along

The whoosh whoosh

Of trees echoing their song

With a pain too strong

To ignore.

Ouch ouch

As they crouch

They shout:

It's not ugly

How dare you cut my bit

Like a worthless piece of meat?

There's no dignity

Or humanity

In a tradition

Where society

Dictates you mutilate

A girl's body!

To prevent promiscuity.

A dark shadow in the Bondo bush

Poised with her BLADE

We can no longer ignore

In this decade

A tradition

I ABHOR

There's no dignity

Or humanity

Where's a girl's sexuality

Is impaired by her MUTILATED body.

Bloody Dowry

Peeping through the veil

A mere child

A flickering smile

Beguiled

Her rage

Innocence bought at a tender age.

Eyes sunken in pain

Tears for the future she'll never regain

Chest swollen

With anguish for a virginity

Stolen

The indignity

of his lust

Contaminating her bust

Her lappa

Conceals her shame.

The blame

Attributed to an abhorrent tradition

Of raping our younger generation

To him, his child-bride

To me, a child defiled.

Can Sierra Leone regain her pride?

Or seal the fate of every child bride?

Find me Mr Right

Had it with the men who spew false promises

Leading you a wild goose chase back home to their missis

Had it with the hot David Beckhams

Enveloping you with their charms

Serenading you with sleezy romantic gibberish

Then dumping you like rubbish

I've been done with the hunky Ashley Coles

Since the start of the last millennium

Their love stories are riddled with holes

I could never de-code their conundrum

While they save up to achieve their goals

You 'll have to deal with debt's pandemonium!

Never had much time for the confident Kanye Wests

Egotism never gave me butterflies

I could see right through their shoddy disguise

Ever since I passed love's eye tests

Had it with being spun around on love's carousel

By posers and losers

Been plunged into the depths of hell

By lovers who were just plain hustlers

Every female psychic can foretell

The good-looking ones morph into bloodsuckers.

Find me Mr Right

A bloke who wears his heart on his sleeve

Not a Lothario lurking in plain sight

Not a romantic pretender

Love's stereotypical Mr Grease

My heart's open to ANY contender

Who's keep its fragile fragments in one piece

The President Came To Tea

The stunning wooden table was exquisitely clad

Mama Salone always hospitable

Laid out all the delicacies she had.

At precisely half past four

THUMP THUMP went the door

The guest's knock was neither gentle

Nor was the hungry stare he bore.

As he approached the table

STOMP STOMP

'What's for dinner?'

'Potato leaves is always a winner'

He sat down with a clump clump

Jeneba twitched her gara lappa

He ungraciously eyed up her buns

He grabbed all their Akara

He scoffed them all at once.

Mama Salone looked with contempt

At his bad-mannered attempt

To eat his potato leaves

smearing all that palm oil on his sleeves

Mama Salone summoned Jeneba to the kitchen

'What were you thinkin?'

Whacking her Egbakoh*

As the guest took a huge mondoh*

Like it was HIS Awujoh*

'Jenaba Isata Passande '

She scolded in Temne

'You''ll forever regret the day

You invited a President to Tea.'

(As Awujoh is a Creole feast An Egbakoh is a wooden spoon used in cooking A mondoh is a large scoop with one's hands).

Hands Off Our Girls

A bevy of national treasure

Our secret power mill

They wear honour as an amour

Sierra Leonean women of steel.

Through the challenges of childhood

Violence and inequality they've stood

Strong, Shrewd and Steadfast

Salone women of valour

were the pillar that did outlast

The ravages of war.

In a land where babies die

A land where women are harassed

And integrous men in short supply.

Our women hold their heads high...

A scholar Benka-Coker

Our mayor Aki-Sawyerr

Our genius Sylvia Blyden

Powerful Sierra Leonean women

Our Auditor Taylor-Pearce

Our women strong and fierce.

Hands off Our Girls

Strong women of substance

Hands off our women of steel

Their Amazonian resistance

Is Sierra Leone's running mill

Hands of our Girls, Maada

Hands off our women of steel

Hands of our power mill.

The fortress

That has been Our Salone buttress

on which we lean

My Hands Off our Girls Campaign

Will immortalize their good name

Climate Catastrophe

Carcasses adorn my village

Where majestic trees once stood

Ravaged By a state-sponsored Savage Trade

In wood.

Our once prestigious

Red Mangrove and African Teak

Plundered week by week

By the State's chosen few.

Salone's stunning woodland

Destroyed by a greedy band

Of our leader's chosen few.

Leadway's leading the timber trade

Of the State's climate charade.

Their green palm tree

An epitome

Of the catastrophe

That's Sierra Leone's climate legacy!

Ode to Lara Taylor-Pearce

Lara,

The truth will shine through deceit

Like an ember in our Sierra Leonean heat

It'll drown out the lies

of the SLPP trojans

With their slogans

And sycophantic cries

Of 'trust the process.'

A camouflage to oppress us

A brigade on a crusade

To LIE…

Lara,

They will trip up on the carpet of our Kenema palm oil

And bury their heads in shame in Lumley's sandy soil...

Lara,

The truth will gush forth like the Guma dam

Re-echoing louder than a Limba drum.

Lara,

Our Kamajors will chase them

back into bushes of oblivion

Unity, Freedom and Justice

Will once more adorn the pavilion

Of our stadium.

Lara,

Sierra Leone will arise from its slumber

A lion roaring like thunder

with the strength of iron Ore.

Devouring corruption to the core.

Wellington fire Tribute

Blazing inferno

Scattering flames

Like upturned raffia baskets

Scatter coins

Fuel spewing from the tanker's loins

Caskets of victims

Unrecognisable

Unidentifiable

Charred bodies on a road

Our hearts a heavy load

of smothering ashes.

A lingering memory

of victims, bed-ridden

Wellington Fire's our President's Wellington

Burnt into our memory

Our leader's scathing history...

<u>Sierra Leone</u>

My child inquired about our history

So I told her this story:

S: is for SHERBRO Island that gave slavery a name

I: stands for INDEGENOUS tie-dying done in Makeni

E: is EBEH my favourite dish!

R: Is for RUTILE that's given us fame

R: is for RONKO a mystical ambiguity

A: is ABERDEEN the home of Fish

L: is for LUNGI'S coastal bay

E: is for EGBAHKOH our wooden spoon

O. is for the OMULLEH we drink on Christmas day

N: is for N'JALA our renowned College

E: is for our forests' EVERGREEN bloom

Every child should hear this story

Of what gives Sierra Leone it's glory.

Take Back Your Dowry

Take Back your Dowry

I don't want you

She chastised

Flashing eyes Like Lightning

striking Our Black Johnson

He's sold.

I don't want you

She bellowed

her stare cold

But words Loud as a Gumbe drum,

Battering his hopes like a Freetown storm.

My riches enticed you

Like palm wine from Pujehun

My diamonds lured you

like the lakes of Kailahun.

I don't know you

She spat with the swish swish of her Shegureh.

Proclaiming''you ain't my Bai Bureh.''

I didn't want this man

Sierra Leone shouted

Brushing him off

With the breeze of her Harmattan.

she departed in disgust

'You haven't earned my trust'

Quivering lips muttered

As he fled:

'I was elected,

I WAS elected,'

He said.

The Lion's Salvation

Sierra Leone's lost

Like a coin

tossed

In the Kangari Hills.

The future fills

us with trepidation.

We're the loin

in an ambush

Trapped in an underbrush

Of corruption.

Will the LIMBA

Pluck up the stamina?

Have the KURANKOH

got the key to the door?

Are the KISSY

Too busy?

Will the YALUNKA

Gush forth like Mano River?

Will the KRIO, the SHERBRO

Muster up the ego?

What will the KRU do?

Can the TEMNE

Defeat this enemy?

Have the LOKO

Got the valour?

Will the MENDE

Pave the way?

Will the FULA, The MADINKA

Or MADINGO, grab Freedom's Charter?

Can we implore

The KONO

To rise up?

Will the SUSU mobilise and stop

The ship of corruption

Docking at Big Wharf?

Which tribe's tough enough

To bring salvation?

Do The Mayor a favour

Pass her, her crown

She's the mother of Freetown.

Her name will be inscribed

In Salone's history

She's ascribed

As a symbol of our victory

Over Ebola.

With her strength of character

She's our victory

Over mediocrity.

With her zeal and pace

Freetown WILL earn a place

As a clean city.

Yvonne Denise Aki-Sawyer

Sierra Leone absolutely adores her!

Pass her, her crown

She's the queen of Freetown.

Riddle of River Rokel

Deep down buried in her sand

Is the anguish

Of children's cries

On her seabed hopes, languish

Her cold rocks are the band

Of the cold-hearted men who cherish

Prepubescent girls.

Her waves batter their innocence

Dreams swept away by her tide

Her sunrise blushes at the abhorrence

Of men's wanton sexual stride.

Her numerous pebbles

Are numerous children

Victims, deaths hidden.

Her breeze whispers her riddle:

'Spirits, tell me why little

girls are wanton toys

Behind closed doors?'

She conjures up her wave

Of feminists

'No more will misogynists

Enslave YOU.

No more will evil win

My river will purge and clean

Away this abominable sin'.

Bumbuna's Blackout

Sierra Leone harbours a darkness

Crevices where light has never shone

The joys of an illuminated happiness

Are ones we've never known.

Plunged into a dam of perpetual blackness

As our leaders lack the backbone

To ignite a surge of passion

One that doesn't emit from Bumbuna alone.

To lead us IN a glowing direction

So, Sierra Leone will transform

Into a bright, blazing beacon of light.

A leader that brings reform

With an electrifying might.

Sierra Leone harbours a darkness

Swamped by a static state of sadness

Minds where lights have never shone

An eternal blackness

That's entirely home-grown.

Wolof Jollof

Slurp slurp

Went the President

Munching on his Jollof

His rice dish was flavoured

With a hint of mouth-watering Wolof.

Beside him host Fatima

Click click went her camera

Flick flick went her hair

The President couldn't have enough

Of his scrumptious Wolof Jollof.

Head chef was Sawaneh

The dish more tantalising than Tempeh

Slurp slurp Went his excellency

Efficiently eating his delicacy

Polishing off the Wolof Jollof with charisma

His feast an enticing enigma

Of Gambia, Kono and Kenema.

Ah aha ah aha

Went his excellency he suddenly began to cough

The meaty concoction was just a bit too tough

Restauranteur Sierra Leone had called his bluff

"Huff Huff"

Roaring in laughter she spat out a rough rebuff

"This meal's banished hunger

I think the President's had enough

never again will our menu offer a Wolof Jollof'.

La Belle Africaine

I'm She…

She with the big bosom

Heaving on a heavy heart

Pulsating with an inner wisdom

Only years of learning can impart

I'm She..

With a vibrating, voluptuous behind

In which joys are intertwined

With jibes, taunts and unkind

Descriptions.

She who in Western perceptions

Ain't a real beauty

With features labelled 'ugly,'

I'm She

With a flared nose

That knows

the pungent smell of decaying dreams

Floating in impoverished African streams.

Full luscious lips

oozing with drips

of salvia from my screams

when abuse ravaged my protruding hips.

I'm She...

Of indescribable purity

Acquired when African rivers cleansed me

My finesse that flows in my veins

Lifts me up from valleys and plains

Unto the rocks of an African Sea

I'm HER

The Black Beauty

In ME.

The incivility of War

Half a limb dangling

An empty life clinging

To a barren tree of hope

Joys of a life fulfilled elope

Me like the sun slips behind the slope

Of Mount Bintumani.

My poignant cries harbour a rhythm

Of the harrowing song of a war-victim

Imploring you to see Me for ME

Not just the amputee.

I'm the symbol of a Sierra Leone

That massacred its own.

Freetown's Fight

Will our historic Cotton Tree

Stir up in me

That passion

That spurred my ancestors into action

That broke the chains of slavery

That steered the ship of bravery

To grab the hope that enhances

That charisma that took chances

To lead up the river that flows

To where we build that dream that grows

From that fight for the freedom and liberty

That founded Freetown, a free city.

The waves at Lumley Beach

(In honour of Kadiatu Kamara, aka KK our only female surfer)

Offshore

A solitary figure

Sliding along the wave

Gliding into its concave

With the elegant skill of the brave.

Transfixed, I watch

Softly the sea-breeze whispers

Sierra Leone will ride the wave

Strength is stashed in her secret coffers

Courage has churned in her coral cave

Together we will OWN the wave.

Contentious census

Frightening fracas

In Tacugama

As the zookeeper begins to count

Contentiously the chimps line up

As cynicism begins to mount.

The apes were expectedly dubious

Of their new animal census.

Then a cheeky Monkey's raucous laughter

Spills out louder than thunder

At the keeper looking all pretentious

Clad all in green; all pompous.

His tone, cold and unconscientious.

Then as the monkeys stare in disbelief

His digital chip fell over the cliff

A baby chimp looked at its mother

And uttered in sheer relief,

'If the keeper wasn't so unstable

His skills so unreliable

That dodgy digital chip

might have ended up in OUR beef'.

Love Died in the war

(A poem for my ex, Daniel Musa who perished in our Civil war).

Shades of bronze

Mingled

In limbs entangled

Your touch

fires up My neurons

Your breath

My breath.

Sizzled

By your brown eyes

Love's bliss elevates us To Freetown's skies.

Passion's force In your kiss

Moves my lips

To exhale piercing cries

As your life slips

Away leaving a core

where pain and dreams are mangled

By miserable memories

Of a ruthless war

That ushered my lover to heaven's door.

<u>That Black Girl</u>

I ain't that girl

With the frizzy curl

You shoved passed on the bus

With your 'she's not one of us'

Snobbish indifference.

The girl on the dating site ranking low in your preference

The black girl on the tube

Who showed no gratitude

When you moved to let her pass?

A chavvy girl with no class

I ain't that girl

Who in your vulgar dreams

dragged you by the seams

Into the realms of erotic fantasy

But who in real life you showed no empathy?

The girl you could date but wouldn't

The girl you could have but didn't

I ain't that girl

With questionable style

You queried in the circumference

of your blind prejudice

Who in popular reference

is tainted by the malice

of the poisoned chalice

Of racism.

I ain't that girl

smeared with the cynicism

of she'll never make the grade

She's a darker shade of the darkest shade

The London lass

From a rundown council estate

The ethnic underclass

That middle class

snobs speculate

Might never rise out of the abyss of poverty

In the highest realms of my fantasy

I'm NOT just that black girl; I am me.

Reflect the real me

In my mirror lives a lady

That isn't the real me

A striking impression

That claims to be me

But this imposter's perfections

don't define me

The real me is inferior

To the lady in the mirror

She wears her insecurities

She doubts her capabilities

She's in no way the extension

Of the stunning reflection

Of the lovely lady

staring back at me

She bears ugly scars

Where life has hurt her

Wrinkles are the memoirs

Of pain beneath her powder

The lady in mirror might flatter

The gullible outsider

But inside me thrives a reminder

That *mirror lady's* just an imposter

A War Memorial

No More No More

Never again that anguish

That tore out our centrepiece

That left hatred to flourish

That reaped the kindness out of kono

That plucked the love out of Port Loko

That masked the beauty of Makeni

That blasted the joy out of Bombali

That built its battleground in Bo

That wiped out unity in Waterloo

That kindled the inferno in Koinadugu

That plucked the pride out of Pendembu

That plagued our lives in Pujehun

That shattered freedom in Freetown

That killed all hope in Kabala

That knobbed a sadness into Kenema

No More No More

Will we stand by or Surrender

To divisions that let hate fluster

When brother turned on brother

When brother tortured brother

No More No More

Will we bleed, perish and groan

As war

Sinks its anchor

into Salone

Sierra Leone, A Rough Diamond

Unpolished

Its glow

concealed below

A layer tarnished

with corruption

A stone flawed

by an inherent quality

A diamond marred

by our dishonesty

Chip away the dust

That smears her gem with rust

Till Sierra Leone's emblem

glistens on her bust.

Christmas Romance

Glistening teeth

Your smile

runs a mile

Along your face

Chiselled arms

Crushing me in the charms

Of your embrace

Flattened abs

Your prize

for a vigorous exercise

Legs of a Gisele

interlock me in your spell

Freetown's finest

Love's own Mr Best

Till distance proved the test

Claiming love as it's conquest

You are a constant distraction

You thrive in my imagination

Your Christmas romance

An enchanting trance

A tease that taunts the rest

Freetown's Mr Best.

Freedom Fled Freetown

Abolition broke our chains

Yet Africa imprisons our brains

Tyrants now abound

Where freed slaves found

A free land.

Sherbro's Shackles

I hear the chains rattling

Where shackles shook your strength

I hear ancient voices wailing

All along your river's length

I see our ancestors hanging

Humans bartered for Tobacco

Your caves were their dungeon

Their tale casts a shadow

On our children yet unborn

An Africa tarnished by European scorn

I hear the Spirituals they're singing

As they toiled in rice fields

I feel their hope wilting

Our lifeblood owns the proceeds

To Great Britain's greatest trade

My blemished history is interwoven in my braid

A tribute to Sherbro's sacrifice

Which my forefathers made

humanity saddest merchandise

A medal that will never fade

32. Leema Had the Hump

Lousy Leema sounded leery

All through Christmas Day

He'd stayed up on Christmas Eve

Downing *Omolleh

He yanked down his garlands

He tossed them in the bin

He unpeeled the *Ollele and ate it with his hands

He picked up the meat skewers and poked

His wife's double-chin

He crushed the CDs of his favourite dance bands

Jumped in the mortar then took the pestle on a spin.

Lousy Leema loudly laughed at choristers

Who came to wish him well

He slammed his door on the carol singers

Told then off for ringing his bell

Playfully pulled faces at the youngsters

Pelted them with Chinese bangers

Then called them 'chubby monsters'

Lousy Leema was so drunk

He took Facebook selfies

And captioned them, 'Salone Hunk'

He cursed at God's son in Heaven

Trumped so loudly it was heard at number seven

Lousy Leema wrecked Sierra Leone's Christmas

With his Yuletide binge

On Leema's Christmas pyjamas

Santa scribbled, 'To the Grinch.'

1. Omolleh is a local alcoholic drink

2. Ollele is a local delicacy

Sabanoh's Classic

Muted voices

Laws bind our tongue

Acquiescing in a deafening silence

Passivity Has sat on our fence

And made democracy A statutory offence

Oppression grows

In our meadows

Tendered by those

Who crawl in others' shadows

Democracy's tunes Are left unsung

Where it's harmony

Synchs all wrong

Not a squeak or murmur in Democracy's defence

Our cowardice has made it

A statutory offence.

Where's Sabanoh's voice coach

Unfaced by tyranny's reproach

To train our voices to sing louder

The melodies of people's power?

<u>Culture War</u>

I lost myself in you

My Creole colours became embedded in your hue

We were the lucky few

Tribalism, status, religion

Hadn't stratified our union

I studied your Fatwa, you drank my Holy Communion

Standing taller than Mount Aureol

Enigmatic presence of a Nomadic angel

My Fulani King

Young love

Blossomed like a flower in spring

Two cultures blended like a hand in glove

I was immersed in you

Till society's customs tainted our emotions

Love usurped by hateful traditions

Our innocence couldn't accrue

The wealth to bribe prejudice's notions

My Maternal Message

Poignant cries

Pierce our ears

From a baby born to die

Mothers' happy smiles belie

The agony of a premature goodbye.

Children chastised For childhood follies

Death threats replace girls' dollies

A promise of a life of poverty

Disguised

In a veil of state secrecy and lies.

Children raised to die

Lives littered with hardship loom

In a future of economic doom

Seeded in our fertile soil of suffering

Sierra Leone's unique offering

To the sacrifice of youth

Youngsters raised to die

Yielding to the wiles of deprivation

Rice served on the plate of starvation

Sierra Leone's on a painful trajectory

To the path that kills posterity

They Call Her Madam Cole

Femi,

Your name's emblazoned

In our roll call of heroes

Your fortitude has impassioned

A new breed of female voters

Femi,

We're with you in Salone's dark abyss

Waiting to swim to peace

A robust boulder in our hurricane

We're leaning on your side

Together we shall all contain

The gigantic wave of corruption.

Sierra Leone's geared up to turn the tide

Femi,

hang in there, Mother

As we ride the turbulent sea

We aren't frightened of its ferociousness

While your gush of wind blows us free

Femi,

We've clasped your grip like a drowning man

To help us stay afloat

Sierra Leone's surrounded you like pebbles

And you're steering our boat

Corruption's waves may swirl and twirl

But in our coral cave of valuables

We've got you, Mother Pearl.

Femi,

You're Sierra Leone's trusted companion

We're comforted by your compassion

You took OUR humiliation

The loving hands that nursed us

Now a mother's hand that guides us

Misogyny's Rainbow

I'm only Ella Jones, not Ella Koblo

My head's not encircled by a halo

Of wisdom

I don't profess to know

All the sages in the Suffragette kingdom

But I know the evil misogyny

Wears a kaleidoscope of colours

Blending deceitfully in harmony

With the sexists amongst us

Masking under popular sentiments

Of a society harbouring resentments

Judged on your looks or virtue

Judged on the men who date you

Society's ethical arbiters of our character

Subject us to constant hate and malicious slander

I frolic with those who don't play

the partisan politics game

I stand with FEMINISTS

who don't victim-blame.

The double standards of a society

Advocating for women's equality

Pretending to see me as Human

Yet underneath their hypocrisy

Thrives a hatred for ME

A woman.

<u>Ode to Leone Stars</u>

Leone Stars Stars in our eyes.

Our hearts a beating Limba drum

Our eyes glued in anticipation

We watch them kicking up a storm

On the football pitch

Awaiting that jubilation…

Sierra Leone's dream team

Having conquered pandemics, we gleam

A brighter future

Never envisaged before

Enlighted by your shining glory

The story Of a nation

undefeatable

Unbelievable

Surprises manifest in our quest to grasp success

As we ascend life's mountains

Our eyes on the summit

We're African Lions; we're strong

Our opponents plumet

On football fields crumbling

Before us

Nonplus

Shocked by our comeback

Sierra Leone's back on track!

Mohamed N Kamara

Umaru Bangura

Mohamed Turay

Leaving rivals in disarray

Steven Caulker

Defensive power

Musa Tombo

Our rainbow

That brightens up our day.

Musa's wife's pure love

Reflects our emotion

Resonating the feeling

We cherish

As we relish

The moment they scored

Delighting fans at home and abroad.

That trepidation

We feel on match day

The anxiety

The Hope

That success once out of scope

Will be Salone's

We're dream swimmers in the Atlantic Ocean

We're mountaineers at Sugar Loaf

We conquer obstacles through strong will

A skill

We aced

Defeating Ebola

Ending our civil war

Stronger than the world gives us credit for

We're Leone Stars

We're Sierra Leone

Freetown Will Be Free

On a freezing cold wintry night

In 1792 ships sailed unto your harbour

Freed Slaves determined to fight

To reach a land of liberty, to grab the tree of hope

Lieutenant John Clarkson our gallant ancestor

Freetown's founder

Sailed from Nova Scotia

Those cargo ships brought him here

To govern a blessed land of slaves

Free, free from racism and discrimination

Free, free from the rationing of Canadian provisions

Where being black was no longer a crime

A forerunner and activist well ahead of his time.

My Black Loyalists forefathers

Are guardian angels of Freetown

Your fervour still flows abundantly in our town

You've impassioned our call for democracy

You drive our stive to advocate for our nation's unity

Black Loyalists bravely battled the turbulent sea

Sailing on hope stronger than boulders

They knew Creole liberty and future

Rested firmly on their strong shoulders

Freetown was rocked on January 6, 1999

In our gruesome civil war

We ploughed through; hatred doesn't define Us.

Unity, Freedom and Justice

Define our coat of arms

Not guns, bullets, or firearms!

Freetonians battled the Ebola pandemic

In a country where poverty is endemic

On the might of our collective power, we soared through

Spurred on by that passion that made Black Loyalists pursue

A realisation of the dream

That all Freetonians dream

To build on the foundations of liberty

That were borne when Europe ended slavery

To grasp the cup of wealth and sip abundantly

That voyage that brought Christianity

That courage that faced calamity

That collective sense of humanity

That love that nurtures nationality

That quest that broke our chains of slavery

That voyage to Freetown's future

When brotherly love and respect for each other's dignity

Become the chains that interlock Freetown's structure

Groundnut Seller

Tray balanced artfully on your head

Shoes worn

from crunching life's shells as you tread

our wretched, rugged, and forlorn

road of destitution

Your groundnut tray of deprivation

Is Impoverishment, balanced on your head

with ease

A skill learned from your mother

An heirloom handed down by your grandmother

A maternal line of misery

Running through our economy

A perpetual curse of poverty

The title of Sierra Leone's story.

Polygamy's Enemy

Love's ghost lives where you once did

Once my epicentre my hub

Consumed by an aching affection

My heart longed to hear yours, throb

Intoxicated by an emotion

Overflowing like unbounded rivers

Your loving touch gave me hot shivers

Love ghost now inhabits your empty chamber

Love's purity tainted by pain

From where daring deception left a stain

A younger wife became my nemesis

My heart evicted from Aphrodite's premises

I plunged into a gaping hole of emptiness

Devoured by a bitterness

When you cheated on love with impunity.

Leaving me on the verge of insanity

www.ellaspoems.co.uk

SIERRA LEONE POEMS

Printed in Great Britain
by Amazon

76604731R00041